Mystic Blade

Gavin Rosenbloom

Published by Gavin Rosenbloom, 2024.

This is a work of fiction. Similarities to real people, places, or events are entirely coincidental.

MYSTIC BLADE

First edition. March 18, 2024.

ISBN: 979-8224560769

Written by Gavin Rosenbloom.

When centuries past, our language will fade
People forget our warnings, and raise their blades
Unspoken horrors for which we have sealed
Will be free, able to roam our fields
We make new allies that we trust with our life
But when night comes, we may meet their knife
Trust vanishes, but can be restored
But love, once gone, there will never be more
Enemies may always be hidden in plain sight
No matter how much faith is in their eyes
When trapped, we may rage like a hog
Then our corpses shall stay, still as a log
Salvation won't come when looking at before
But when gazing at tomorrow, our power will grow ever more

Kingdom of Deinceps, July 15th, 1605;

Alexander, the Miner worked. For hours, he mined, digging up valuable resources for his Kingdom. At home, he lived alone. He would write poems for fun. Alexander was a kind person. He often puts others before himself. He was well liked among many people for his charming personality, and good sense of humor. Alexander was 177 centimeters tall, with brown hair, a sharp chin, and hazel eyes. Deincaps was a relatively small kingdom located right in between France and Switzerland. Despite its small size, Deincaps was extremely rich in culture and in wealth. Deincaps was covered in tall mountains and beautiful lush forests.

One day, Alexander woke up, and left for work. When he got there, he saw his friend, Erwin. Him and Erwin talked for a while. They talked about work, politics, but mostly, about poems. They had known each other since they were children, yet they always had that common interest. They soon got to work at the Mines. For hours, they mined resources to give to their kingdom. While mining, they would tell each other stories. Stories about love, about hatred, about freedom. Erwin was the only person close to Alexander. Alexander's parents died when he was too young to remember, and was brought to an orphanage, where he met Erwin. They were there for each other through thick and thin. Erwin was slightly shorter than Alexander, with blonde hair and a more round chin.

One day, in the mines, Alexander hit something hard, a metal. But it was purified, almost artificial. Alexander called over Erwin to look at it. Erwin and Alexander dug out the entire thing, it was a sword. It was made of hardened steel, forged to perfection. Its handle was wrapped in strips of leather. The words "BLADE OF DEATH" were carved into the blade. Shocked and mesmerized by this discovery, Erwin accidentally cut his finger on the edge. Suddenly, he fell to the floor unconscious. Alexander checked his pulse to see that, somehow, he had died. Black mist started pouring from his mouth. In terror, he grabbed the sword, but when he did, something mysterious happened. He heard screaming. He turned around to see the whole Mine filled with the black mist. And in it, he saw creatures appearing.

The creatures looked almost human, but their skin was pitch black, and was melting off. Their limbs long, yet slender. Their eyes like endless voids. The image haunted Alexander as he ran out of the Mine with the sword. When he got out, he fell to his knees. He looked at the sword with terror, and confusion. He felt sick in his stomach. *What were those monsters?* Alexander thought to himself. Suddenly, his vision became blurry, and his ears started ringing. And then, he fell unconscious. He woke up with his hand tied on a pole behind him. He looked up to see 5 people sitting on thrones above him

Chapter One: A Journey's Start

"Where am I?" He said after a brief moment of trying to compose himself.

"You are in the presence of the Council." One said. "We are in charge of all sorcery and relics, including the sword you have found.

"The sword? What even is it?" Said Alexander

"That sword is from a time, hundreds of years ago." Said the Council member. "It's obvious you don't know the history, so let me explain it to you. Hundreds of years ago, Sorcery was the dominating force in the world. Those who could harness it were the strongest of humanity. But there was one person who changed this, a sorcerer by the name of Castellan. After a spell went wrong, it corrupted his soul, and gave him an unrelenting thirst for blood. And so he developed his own form of sorcery called Dark Sorcery. Dark Sorcery allowed him to absorb the Life Energy of any being he killed. He started murdering every sorcerer that he crossed paths with. Before long, he was the most powerful being in the world. He soon became so powerful, he made himself immortal, completely unable to die no matter what happened to him. But soon one sorcerer had thought of a plan to defeat him. He gathered the strongest sorcerers left, and made a Relic, an object infused with sorcery. Together, they created the Blade Of Death, a sword with the ability to instantly kill anything it cut in the slightest. Although Castellan was Immortal, the sword still did severe damage. Instead of killing him, the sword knocked him unconscious for 24 hours. After successfully cutting him, the council trapped Castellan in a prison, and lodged the sword into his body, keeping him unconscious forever so long as the sword was in his body. The founder of the Council developed a spell to stop himself from aging to ensure sorcery was never used for war again. 500 years later, he is still alive, and he is me. My name is Heinrich."

Alexander looked up at the man. He didn't look 500, he looked closer to 40. He was bald, around 165 centimeters. He had a friendly appearance, and a strong German accent.

"But if Castellan is unconscious for 24 hours after being stabbed, how did he immediately use sorcery after the sword was removed?" Said Alexander.

"We believe that somehow, his power has strengthened within the 500 years he was unconscious, whilst the sword's power had weakened." Said Heinrich.

"That's enough. You are not here to ask questions." Another Council member said.

Alexander looked over to see the Council member. She was short, around 157 centimeters, with brown curly hair. Her eyes were Aqua. From the first chance you could assume she was a teenager, but despite that, she had a fierce look on her face. She was fierce, strong, yet sarcastic.

"Frieda, please don't be so rude to our guest." Said Heinrich.

"Guest?" Said Frieda. "He stole the Blade Of Death, freeing Castellan from his prison."

"You know the public has no knowledge of sorcery, he couldn't possibly have known the consequences of his actions." Said Heinrich.

"Is she usually this grumpy?" Said Alexander.

"I'm sorry, this was a poor way to introduce you two." Said Heinrich. "Alexander, this is Frieda, our weaponry expert. She is in charge of the use of sorcery in conflict."

"I can tell she's not the public image of your Council." Said Alexander

"The hell did you just say about me?" Said Frieda. "If it was up to me, you would be in the ground right now."

"You were going to kill me because I didn't know about the sword?" Said Alexander. "Are you insane?"

Frieda raised her hand, like she was about to slap him. Suddenly her fingernails unraveled into a sort of String.

"Frieda, that's enough!" Yelled Heinrich. Suddenly, there was a bright, dark blue light emitted from Heinrichs hand. The strings coming from Frieda's hands suddenly retracted, turning back into her fingernails. Frieda looked surprised, and livid.

"Please forgive Frieda." Said Heinrich. "Please don't blame her for her attitude, she has suffered more than you could ever imagine. You see, when she was a child she was exposed to intense magic."

While Henrich spoke, Frieda swung her arms furiously, and groaned in anger.

"It gave her the ability to unravel her fingernails into a string that she can control. However, that ability comes at a cost. Every second she isn't using her ability, she's in pain. Though she can hide it, she can't erase it." Said Heinrich.

"I'm so sorry, I had no idea her life was like that." Said Alexander. "But what did you do to her?"

"I temporarily revoked her powers, so she wouldn't hurt you. The threads her fingernails turn into are hard as steel, and sharp as a razor. If she swung them at you, it would severely injure you." Said Heinrich.

“If you can revoke her powers, why didn't you do that as soon as she got them?” Said Alexander.

“I can only take them away temporarily,” said Heinrich, “her powers are infused with her soul, and the soul is the one thing sorcery cannot touch at all. I can temporarily make her unable to use them, but I can't truly take them away.”

"My sincerest apology for what I said to you." Said Alexander. He looked at Frieda with pity, and guilt. Although it was only a few seconds Alexander stared at her, it felt like minutes to him.

Another Council member started laughing. Alexander looked over at him. He was tall, with a deep voice. He had a smirk on his face.

"Alexander, you know we all know what you're thinking, right?" He said.

Alexander was embarrassed, and quickly tried changing the subject of the conversation.

"Well, it's about time you get started with your mission." Said Heinrich.

“What mission?" Asked Alexander.

"Since you freed Castellan, it's only natural that it's your responsibility to defeat him." Said Heinrich.

"Defeat him?" Said Alexander. "I can't do sorcery, I don't have any experience with any weapons, I'm just a Miner, not a warrior. How should I defeat him by myself?"

"You will not be alone. Frieda will assist you." Said Heinrich.

Frieda was shocked. She didn't want to be with Alexander. She tried convincing Heinrich to send someone else, but Heinrich wouldn't budge.

"And about training," said Heinrich. "There's a training facility about 2 miles Northwest of here. You and Frieda should head there now to get started with training."

"But still, why not give the sword to someone who already has years of sword training? I've never even touched one until now." Said Alexander.

"The sword has a locking mechanism on it. When someone wields it, they're stuck with it till death. If anyone else tries to hold it, they'll die. When you grabbed the sword, it locked. Until you die, anyone else who grasps the sword will instantly die." Explained Heinrich.

Alexander was freed from his restraints, and was given his sword back, along with a sheath. Him and Frieda began the long walk to the training facility. During the walk, Alexander tried sparking conversation with Frieda, but she responded with nothing but sarcastic and rude comments. Alexander knew that if they were to work together, they would have to get along, yet Frieda clearly was upset about the situation.

"So, do you have any family?" Asked Alexander.

"I did, but thanks to you, they're dead by now." Said Frieda, with a sad, low voice.

"What do you mean?" Asked Alexander.

"If you must know, I had a loving family. A mom, dad, and two sisters." She said, "When I was 5, I fell into a cave. In front of me, there were 8 massive stones, each with glowing runes carved into them. I touched one, but that was a mistake. It filled my body with magic, giving me powers, but putting me in unending pain. When my parents found me in the cave, I couldn't stop screaming from the pain. My parents stayed by my side no matter what. When I joined the Council, we couldn't see each other, but we sent letters, almost every day. But now, they're gone."

Tears started to form on Frieda's face, and her voice got sadder.

> "We lived in a small town, right by a large mine. By the mine you worked at, where Castellan was set free, where his rampage has begun. If they didn't evacuate the moment you set him free, he's got to them by now. But what he does to his victims is cruel. He corrupts their bodies, then their souls. He strips them of all their thoughts, feelings, and free will, turning them into nothing but mindless killing machines we call Husks. And the damage is irreversible, there's no way to free people from his grasp. And once Castellan dies, all under his control also die."

Frieda broke down crying. Alexander didn't know how to react. He had seen what was beyond the ferocious shell Frieda had displayed, a young girl denied a childhood, simply wanting to help her family. He felt unbearable guilt knowing that he was responsible for the deaths of Frieda's family, for his best friend, and for everyone else ruthlessly attacked by Castellan. He knew that no matter what, he must atone for his actions by killing Castellan.

"I swear on my life I will fix this." Alexander said. Frieda's sobbing continued, but Alexander could tell she was listening. "I too, have already lost someone close to me to Castellan. But now, we're being given a chance to avenge the fallen, and prevent this from happening to anyone else."

Frieda's sobbing stopped, as she seemed fully captivated by Alexander's words. "This is our one and only chance to kill Castellan, will you help me?" Alexander said, kneeling down and putting his right hand on Frieda's shoulder.

Frieda chuckled. "That meltdown was very childish of me, I apologize." She said.

Alexander also chuckled. "Listen, I know this is my fault, and I don't expect you to forgive me-"

"-No, it's not." Frieda interrupted. "It's like Heinrich said, there's no way you could've known about sorcery, and thus that taking that sword would have these consequences. If we can pin the blame on anyone, it should be on us in the Council for not taking further measures to prevent his return."

"I'm glad you've forgiven me," Alexander said, "but don't expect me to give up on killing Castellan now. If anything, I'm more motivated now."

Frieda reached out her hand for Alexander to grab. "Let's kill him together." She said.

"Together." Alexander repeated, grabbing her hand.

Throughout the rest of the walk, Frieda was much more open to Alexander. She talked to him about her life, her experiences in the Council.

"So who was that one Council Member that said he knew what I was thinking?" Asked Alexander.

"Oh, that's Thomas." Said Frieda. "He's in charge of creating and managing all the Relics."

"What are Relics?" Asked Alexander.

"Relics are objects infused with sorcery." Explained Frieda. "There are these things called Totems, they are small glowing blue marbles. Using sorcery, they can be implanted into any object, but the process of fusing an object with a Totem is incredibly difficult. Only Thomas and Heinrich can do it."

Alexander felt at peace there, even with the circumstances. The Council buildings beautiful design helped with this sense of peace. It was a large campus, 5 miles in radius, centered around one building. In this campus, there were several large buildings, each serving a different purpose. Each building was made of oak wood and marble. There was a forest just outside the campus, but that didn't obstruct the view of the gorgeous snow-capped mountains. Eventually, Alexander and Frieda got to the training field. There, he saw Thomas waiting for him. Then began Alexander's training. For the next few months, everyday for hours and hours, Thomas taught Alexander how to fight with a sword. While Alexander was training, the council sent armies of sorcerers to help fight Castellan.

Despite being trained with a sword, Thomas did not fight with one. Instead, he fought with another Relic. It was a mace with numerous magical abilities. Its chain could extend up to a mile's length. And it could hit with enough flip over a small island. Along with sword training, Heinrich taught Alexander how to use Sorcery.

"All sorcery is derived from things known as Runes." Said Heinrich. "Runes are like letters of the alphabet, but they're much more than that. One Rune by itself does nothing, but when you pair them together, they can do tasks. The more Runes you put together, the more complex things you can do. But casting Runes comes at a cost. Whenever you cast Runes, you use your own life force, and if you run out, you die."

"So if you use Sorcery too much, it can kill you?" Said Alexander.

"Yes. But you also lose life force when you are injured. That's why you shouldn't use Sorcery too recklessly, or when you are injured. But you only use life force depending on the amount of Runes you use, and the scale of the spell you cast. That's why you should always find ways to use the smallest amount of Runes as possible. But apart from that, Sorcery has endless possibilities, and it can let you change anything anywhere in the world. If you can imagine it, there's a spell to do it, whether that's changing an object's size, shooting a fireball from your hands, bringing life to inanimate objects, or even stopping the Earth's orbit."

Alexander was trained in sorcery, yet couldn't use it. Everytime he tried to use sorcery, he suddenly saw the image of the creature Erwin had turned into, and it haunted him. He fell to the ground in terror, every time. Despite that, things were looking bright for Alexander. He became skilled with a sword. He learned an ancient fighting style based on the movements of a bat. It relies on quick, agile movements instead of raw power. However, things soon started falling apart.

One day, a dark cloud appeared above the Council. Heinrich looked terrified, as he knew what this cloud meant. Suddenly, lightning struck the floor in front of them. And there stood, Castellan.

"It's been so, so long, Heinrich." Castellan said." I can tell time has done you no good. You have been weakened to barely a fraction of your original strength. Yet in those 500 years, I have been absorbing the magic of the Blade. Whilst your strength diminished, mine grew."

Alexander and Frieda were at the training facility when it happened. In one moment, everything was peaceful. In the next, chaos began. Frieda looked up to the sky, to see it blocked by a giant black cloud, all circling around the council's main headquarters. She quickly ran towards it, and Alexander soon followed.

Thomas readied his weapon to fight Castellan, yet he laughed.

"Do you really think you have any hope of defeating me?" Castellan said. "Your only hope of even scratching me is the Blade Of Death, yet it's miles away at the moment."

"How do you know where it is?" A shocked Heinrich said.

'Every battle is won before it's ever fought." Said Castellan. "That is something Sun Tzu said. Do you know what it means? It means that you should observe your opponents and plan accordingly if you wish to be victorious. That's why I studied the new council, and the Blades new wielder. And I waited until I grew in numbers, and in strength to attack. Finally, I waited until the blade was far away from you all before I attacked. Now, not only is the Blade miles away, but only three of the Council members are here, one of them being with the Blade."

"Enough!" Yelled Thomas, as he threw his mace towards Castellan. Even with the spiked ball flying faster than sound, Castellan effortlessly caught it with one hand. The ground behind Castellan was completely shattered, like a piece of glass against a boulder.

"That's impossible." Exclaimed Thomas. Suddenly, a black tentacle appeared from Castellan's back. It was made of a black smoke. The tentacle lunged towards Thomas, and it stabbed him. Thomas fell to the floor, his pupils vanished, and his breathing faint.

"No!" Yelled Heinrich. He ran towards Thomas, but before he reached him, Castellan's tentacle lunged towards Heinrich. But before the tentacle could get close, there was some sort of loud rumbling. Suddenly, the ground tore apart. Stone that was buried deep underground quickly zipped to the surface, blocking the tentacle's path to Heinrich. As the tentacle hit the stone, it shattered the stone and then disappeared. This is the power of Heinrich.

Alexander and Frieda arrived at the scene, horrified. The ground was ripped to shreds, Thomas laying in a pool of his blood, and Castellan standing there, menacingly. Castellan turned his head and looked towards Alexander. His meer glance sent shivers down Alexander's spine. Then, Castellan glanced at the blade with delight.

"Alexander, at last we meet." Castellan yelled with delight. "I must respect the amount of effort you have put into your training, to kill me.

The blade is in good hands with you. But now, you will hand it over to me."

Alexander looked at Castellan fearfully. Castellan was 213 centimeters tall. His skin looked dry and rotten, it had been corrupted by Dark Sorcery. The whites of his eyes were pitch-black, and his pupils were crimson. His death stare was so intense that a wild tiger would whimper in fear if he glanced at it.

"And why would I do that?" Asked Alexander.

"If you hand over the blade, I will let you go. "Said Castellan. "You can flee Deinceps and run off to England or France, wherever you please. You will be spared from my wrath. But if you refuse, I will turn you into a Husk."

Alexander glanced over at Frieda, who was trembling in fear and in anger. He unsheathed the blade, and got into a fighting stance. "Very well then." Said Castellan as he summoned another tentacle. The Tentacle lunged at Alexander, faster than the blink of an eye, but Alexander dodged it even faster. The tentacle hit the ground with immense force, and then disappeared. Two more appeared, And Alexander held his blade at an angle towards one. As it hit him, the force knocked him back, away from the other one. Five more appeared, and Alexander dodged all of them. *Quick, agile, unpredictable.* Alexander repeated to himself in his head. *If I wish to survive, that is how I must move.*

“Very impressive!” Exclaimed Castellan. In what seemed like an instant, Alexander was behind Castellan. He swung the blade at Castellan with all the strength he could muster. And as it hit Castellan, nothing happened. Castellan's skin was too tough for Alexander to cut through. Castellan laughed, and then launched a counter-attack. He swung his arm at Alexander with so much force that the Earth shook, and with so much speed that Alexander just barely managed to dodge it. Castellan pulled his arm back to punch Alexander, but Frieda suddenly wrapped her threads around Castellan's arm. He looked at the threads, and laughed. And with a slight nudge of his arm, Frieda was sent flying a few meters into the air. She hit the ground with a sprained wrist, but got back up and ran straight at Castellan. She unraveled the threads again, and swung them at Castellan. But the razor sharp threads could not pierce his skin. Castellan grasped the threads, and yanked them, thrusting Frieda back at him. But before she reached him, Alexander mustered the strength to cut the threads. But Frieda's momentum kept her flying towards Castellan, Alexander quickly tackled Frieda out of the air. But as they hit the ground together, Alexander dropped the blade.

Castellan ran to grab the blade. But before he could reach it, the ground suddenly ripped apart beneath it, and the rubble suddenly gathered in a sphere around it. Castellan looked over to see Heinrich using his sorcery to protect the blade. But suddenly, Thomas awokend. He swung his flail at Heinrich. Heinrich used sorcery to stop the flail mid-air, but it still had enough force to knock him back without hitting him directly. Heinrich was sent flying into the air. Heinrich was severely injured. Several of his ribs were broken, and his arm was dislocated. The spell Heinrich had casted to protect the Blade was released.

Alexander was filled with rage. He wanted nothing but to kill Castellan there and then. *How am I supposed to kill this asshole if he's immortal?* Alexander thought to himself. Besides, neither the blade nor Frieda's threads did anything to Castellan, they didn't even scratch him. Alexander looked over to Frieda, he could tell she was thinking the same. There's no way they could defeat this nigh-omnipotent being, they had to flee. Alexander quickly began sprinting towards the Blade to flee with it, but Castellan also began sprinting towards it. Alexander was already exhausted from the fight, and he had twisted his ankle when he fell, but he had to power through it. He mustered all the remaining strength he had to reach the sword before Castellan.

As Alexander ran, there was suddenly a loud boom, and the air shook violently. Alexander could feel the bones in his legs splintering, but he had to power through the pain, for if he slowed down at all, Castellan would get the sword. The pain became unbearable for Alexander.

Although he had not even ran for a second, it felt like years. But soon, he reached the sword. Alexander fell to the ground, with the sword in his hands. Alexander tried to stand, but couldn't. He had pushed himself too far, and it shattered his legs. Castellan looked down at Alexander, and laughed.

"You may have gotten the sword before me, but in your current state, you can't go on any further." Said Castellan. Suddenly, Castellan punched Alexander. The ground was ripped to shreds with the immense force, and the cloud of dust was blinding. But as the dust cloud cleared, Castellan noticed something bizarre. There was no blood, not a single drop. And Alexander's body was nowhere to be found. Castellan looked back to see Frieda, with both Alexander and Heinrich in her arms. She managed to wrap her threads around them, and pull them back towards her. Castellan ran toward them, in anger. But before Castellan reached them, Heinrich reached out his hand. "Begone!" Heinrich yelled, as a burst of golden light erupted from his hand. And suddenly, Castellan was gone. But because Heinrich used Sorcery with his injuries, he suddenly fell unconscious.

Heinrich woke up. He looked around, he was in a cave with Alexander and Frieda. "Finally, you're awake!" Exclaimed Alexander." Heinrich sat up. He looked around the cave to see a small fire, some medical supplies, the Blade in its sheath leaning against a wall near the fire, and Frieda pacing around the cave, her face red from anger and fear.

"How long was I asleep?" Asked Heinrich.

"Three days." Said Alexander. "So that spell you used on Castellan, what was that?"

"A containment spell." Said Heinrich. "I trapped him in another world. But unfortunately, the spell doesn't last very long, only about 30 minutes."

What do we do? What do we do! Frieda muttered to herself.

"If what Castellan said was right, the Blade will longer do anything to him." Said Alexander.

"I know." Heinrich said softly.

"How can we defeat him without the sword? Isn't it impossible?" Said Alexander.

"Not exactly." Said Heinrich. "There is still a bit of hope."

"Like what? Talking him out of Omnicide?" Snapped Freida, her voice filled with fear.

"No," Said Heinrich. "There's something I've been hiding from you, and everyone else in the council."

Alexander and Frieda both looked over towards Heinrich with confusion.

"There are dozens of different types of sorcery. I use one called Omnipotence, which focuses on controlling the different colored energies. Castellan uses Dark Sorcery which focuses on stealing the life energy of the people he kills. But there's another type of Sorcery, one so powerful that one who can use it may be called a God, Time Control."

"Time Control?" Both Freida and Alexander said simultaneously.

"Yes. It's a powerful type of Sorcery that can control the flow of time, or an object or person's position in it." Said Heinrich. "One of its abilities is to reset a thing to a state it was at in the past, meaning-"

"-You could reset Castellan to before he learned Dark Sorcery, stripping away his Immortality." Alexander interrupted.

"Exactly." Said Heinrich "but learning Time Control will not be easy. You could spend your whole life studying it, yet only scratch the surface of it. Are you sure you devote the rest of your life to learning it? Time Control takes a hefty amount of Life Energy from its user, which my 500 year old body doesn't have. And Frieda's ability prevents her from using Sorcery of any kind, so neither of us can do it for you, but I can teach it to you."

“Whatever it takes, I will do it!” said Alexander.

For the next few months, Alexander studied Time Control with Heinrich. He had previously tried to learn Omnipotence, yet Alexander could never use it. But they thought Time Control would be different.

Alexander was much more determined to learn Time Control, and he had more of a reason to learn it. Yet he still could not use it. He memorized all the techniques, abilities, everything there is to know about it, yet couldn't use it. Like knowing how to run freely, but having no legs. One day, Alexander collapsed, with a look of utter defeat on his face.

"It's hopeless." muttered Alexander. Time Control was our only hope of defeating Castellan, yet I can't use it."

"No, it's not over yet." Said Heinrich. "When me and the original council defeated Castellan, we knew that there was a chance he could be released, so we made plans for a Relic that could almost completely nullify Dark Sorcery. We call it, 'the Mystic Veil.'"

"Where is this Relic?" Asked Alexander.

"It hasn't been built yet, we simply have made the plans." Said Heinrich.

"Then how do we make it?" Asked Alexander.

"All you need to do is bring me a Totem, and I'll do the rest." Said Heinrich. "The nearest totem is located about 50 miles from here, in a small village named 'Eichenfelden.'

Alexander grabbed the Blade and its sheath, and latched them onto his belt. "We'll begin our journey there now." He declared.

Chapter Two: Embark

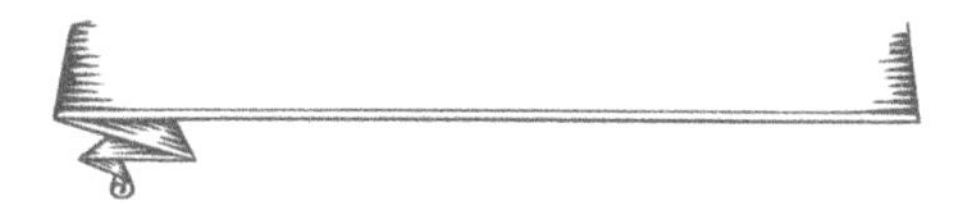

Frieda stomped out the fire they had set, as Alexander gathered their belongings. Heinrich gathered a gold energy in his hands, and shaped it into an orb. He grabbed a nearby lantern, and stuffed it into the orb, before the orb disappeared. As Alexander and Frieda finished their tasks, Heinrich pointed in the direction of Eichenfelden, as they began their expedition. They walked through the forest for an hour before coming across a small town. All three of them were tired, and hungry. So they decided to stop by the bar to get fed and rested.

As they walked into the bar, they were immediately hit with a foul stench, which bothered Frieda more than the others. As they walked to the counter, Frieda was bothered by the stench and the noise, Alexander was bothered by the fear of losing the blade in there, and Heinrich was bothered by all the people's ignorance of the crisis. They made it to the counter, found seats, ordered their food, and waited. But as they waited, a large man approached Frieda, which she noticed from the corner of her eye.

"Can I help you?" Frieda said sarcastically.

"Now what is your business here?" Said the man, with a cocky look on his face.

"Oh, wouldn't you like to know." Said Frieda, arrogant as ever.

The man slammed his hand on the table, furious at Frieda's reaction to his question. He attempted to threaten Frieda, but was even more furious when she dismissed him as if he were just an angry child. The man then attempted to punch Frieda, but in an instant, she flew off her chair, and dodged the punch. The man attempted to throw three more punches, all of which Frieda dodged with ease. But before he could make another attempt, Alexander got in between them.

"Back off, now." Alexander said with a serious tone of voice. "Just look at her, she's too weak for you to fight." Alexander put his hand on the Blade, and pulled it out just enough to reveal the shine of the Blades sharp edge. The man quickly shoved Alexander out of the way, and grabbed a dagger hidden beneath his coat. He charged towards Frieda, only for her to disarm him, and pin him to the ground in only a second. The man ran off. As they left the bar, Heinrich placed his hand on Alexander's shoulder, then slapped him.

"What the hell were you thinking?" Yelled Heinrich. "You cannot pull the sword out on normal citizens under any circumstances! What if you had been arrested? You would either have to abandon our mission, or escape police custody, and become a fugitive of the kingdom. And if you had actually used the blade, the public would now know about sorcery."

"I apologize." Said Alexander. "I was furious seeing Frieda being threatened, and I was overcome by anger."

"That is your issue!" Yelled Heinrich. "You let your emotions act for you. You must learn to overcome your emotions, or we **will** fail our mission."

Frieda suddenly unraveled her fingernails, and swung her arm at the forest around her. Several tall trees instantly fell to the ground in pieces. "I don't need your protection." She said. Frieda didn't seem mad, but insulted. She was insulted by Alexander's assumption that she was weak. Although Alexander simply was helping her, she felt as if he had assumed that she was weak without her powers, and needed protection. As the large chunks of wood fell to the ground, birds flew away, and the uprooted dirt polluted the air. "I don't need anyone."

As they continued their journey, they were silent. But despite their silence, they all had many thoughts racing through their minds. They walked through the forest, and soon reached a river. To cross the river, they walked along an old, creaky bridge. The bridge was in horrible shape. It had mold growing over it, broken planks of wood, and the metal screws were rusted. Alexander looked into the water. Just underneath this old creaky bridge, was beautiful water. The rocks that rested in the water all sparkled as if they were metal. The rocks were all large, about the size of a man's head, except for one rock that had been shattered into bits. Alexander watched as the water carried away the debris from the shattered rock. Across the river, there was just more forest. All of the trees stood tall, with branches that stretched out and covered the sky. The only bit of sky visible was from a broken path of branches. Despite these beautiful sights, the group remained quiet, but their silence was interrupted by a loud bang. And there stood a 20 meter tall giant.

"Impossible," exclaimed Heinrich. "Giants have been gone for five centuries. How could one appear now?"

"This could be the work of Castellan?" asked Alexander.

But before they could talk anymore, Frieda rushed towards the Giant. She felt she had to prove her strength, and what better way then to take down a giant single handedly? Alexander attempted to rush in to help her, but Heinrich held him back. "Let her do this." Heinrich said. Alexander stepped back, clearly worried about Frieda, but understanding her strength.

The Giant swept its arm across the floor in an attempt to crush Frieda, which Frieda effortlessly dodged by jumping. The Giant lifted its hand, and smashed it on the floor, Frieda simply moved out of the way. As the Giant wound its arm back for another punch, Frieda wrapped her threads around its arm, and the momentum launched her into the air.

Alexander looked towards the fight with terror in his eyes. Every instinct in his body was telling him that Frieda was in danger, and he needed to save her. However, his trust in her strength and Heinrichs judgment to not interfere held him back, so he only stood by and watched his fear. Heinrich was also terrified of what might happen, yet he hid it from Alexander.

Once she flew behind the Giant, she cut into its shoulder with her threads. The Giant yelled out in pain, and attempted to punch Frieda. Frieda threw her threads at the Giants feet, and wrapped them around its ankle. She pulled on the threads, moving her out of the way of the punch. Once she reached the ground, she rolled in order to disperse the force of the impact. She then pulled on the threads to tighten them so much to the point that the Giants foot came off. The Giant fell to the ground, unable to stand.

Frieda pulled her hand behind her, and quickly swung it in front of her. Her threads moved at the Giant, so fast that they decapitated it. The Giant was slain. This beast that would normally take entire armies to defeat was taken down in less than a minute by Frieda, and Frieda alone. Frieda looked towards Alexander and Heinrich, with a look in her eyes that demanded praise. “It is done,” she said, “The Giant is dead. Through my strength alone, a Giant has fallen.”

Heinrich stepped towards Frieda. “You have done well.” He said. “You have proven that your strength far exceeds any normal man or woman."

Alexander walked towards Frieda, and hugged her. "I'm sorry," he said, "I was wrong to judge your strength back at the bar. After losing my best friend Erwin all those years ago, I was terrified. I didn't want to lose you as well."

“No, you were just trying to protect me.” Said Frieda. “It's my fault for being so damn sensitive. When I got my curse for the first time, I coped with the pain by convincing myself that I was the strongest there is. I told myself that none could stand up to me, not even God himself. That's why having my strength questioned always hurts so badly.”

“I'm glad we've both recovered from this,” Alexander said, “remember, we agreed to work together to kill Castellan. Now, let's not let anything else get in the way.”

With their mended relationship, the group continued on their journey. They soon exited the forest, and came across another bridge. It had been recently built, or repaired. It was in almost perfect conditions. There were no broken planks, and the metal screws almost shined. But Frieda noticed something, black smoke coming from a nearby village. The group instantly recognized this smoke, it was the smoke that Castellan made. They rushed to the village, to find it completely overrun with Castellan's Husks.

Chapter Three: Insanity

One of the Husks noticed them, and quickly rushed towards them. Alexander grabbed the Blade, but couldn't unsheathe it. He found his mind flooding with the image of Erwin, and the monster he was turned into. Erwin had been turned into one of these creatures that he was about to kill, and Alexander couldn't get that thought out of his head. As the creature approached Alexander, Heinrich killed it by making a spike from the ground to impale it. Frieda placed her hand on Alexander's shoulder, and slapped him.

"Why can't you fight?" She asked. Though Alexander didn't say anything verbally, the look in his eyes told Frieda everything she needed to know. "These creatures aren't humans anymore. Their minds and bodies are corrupt. They have no will, no emotions, no thoughts."

"Erwin..." mumbled Alexander, "Any one of these things could be Erwin. How could I bring myself to kill him? It wouldn't be right."

A few more Husks spotted the group, and began charging towards them. "I trust that you'll pull yourself together." Frieda said as she got into a fighting stance. As the Husks approached, Frieda and Heinrich prepared to attack. But in just a second, they all fell to the ground, lifeless. And in front of their corpses stood Alexander with the Blade in his hand, and tears in his eyes. Alexander spotted a few more Husks, and quickly killed them. Alexander watched as the Husks corpses hit the floor and instantly dissolved into a black dust, as if they never existed. No matter how hard the group tried, there were always more Husks, charging towards them. As the group fought, they tried to think of a plan. They couldn't keep fighting forever, but they couldn't abandon the village either. But their planning was interrupted by a scream, one from a villager.

"You keep holding back the Husks, I'll go get the villagers to safety." Said Alexander.

"Okay, but be quick," Said Heinrich, "We can't hold the Husks back for much longer."

Alexander ran towards the direction of the scream. He encountered more Husks along the way, and killed them with ease. "Is anyone there!?" Alexander yelled. "Help!" The voice cried out again. Alexander was now close enough to the villager screaming for him to locate where it was coming from, a house right next to him.

Alexander broke down the door, only to find the house completely barren. He spotted a staircase, and went up it to find the villager. It was a short, blonde girl. She was young, presumably around 15.

"There you are!" Alexander said with a feeling of relief. "Are you hurt?"

"No, I'm okay." The girl said.

"Where are your parents?" Alexander asked.

"I don't know." She said with fear in her voice. "One moment, everything was alright. But suddenly, lightning struck, and a tall man appeared. Tentacles appeared from his back, and they stabbed my parents. And then..." tears started flowing from the girl's eyes.

"Don't worry, I'll get you out of here." Said Alexander. Alexander was confused. *If the girl's parents were turned into Husks, why was she alright? And why weren't they in the house?* Alexander thought to himself. But this wasn't the time for questions. *She was probably just hiding from the Husks* Alexander thought to himself.

"Are there any other villagers here?" Asked Alexander.

"No, I'm the only one." The girl said.

Alexander sheathed the Blade, and picked the girl up. He ran back towards Frieda and Heinrich to tell them what had happened. With the only remaining villager, they fled. They camped at a small cave to treat their wounds, and recharge from the fight. Alexander and the girl sat down next to each other.

"What's your name?" Alexander said.

"I'm Kayla." She said.

"I'm Alexander, and they are Frieda and Heinrich. We're here to kill the man who destroyed your village." Alexander said.

Kayla had a shocked look on her face, before asking Alexander another question, "What are you going to do now?"

Alexander was surprised by this comment. It made him realize, how are they supposed to kill Castellan if they can't save one village? He stood up, and went to talk with Frieda and Heinrich. They stood in a circle to discuss their plan while Kayla sat on the floor behind Heinrich. But as Heinrich was about to speak, he suddenly gasped, and fell to the floor. They looked at Heinrich, there was a knife wound in his back. Then they looked at Kayla, holding a bloodied knife.

"You bastard!" Frieda yelled, as she unraveled her threads, and swung them at Kayla. But suddenly, Kayla appeared behind Frieda. She was about to stab Frieda, but Alexander swung the Blade at Kayla, forcing her to back away. Just a minute ago, Kayla seemed terrified, like an animal trapped in a cage. But now, she was laughing hysterically, and she was grinning from ear to ear.

"You idiots!" Kayla yelled. "I can't believe you actually trusted me. You actually thought I was just a little defenseless girl in the village. No, if that was the case, I would've been the first to die from those Husks!"

"Why are you doing this?" Asked Alexander.

"I can't let you kill my lord, Castellan." She yelled. "He promised me the world if I killed you."

"You can't trust Castellan." Said Alexander. "He lied to you, he's just gonna use you, and then kill you!"

The smirk suddenly disappeared off Kayla's face, and was replaced by a face of pure anger. "How dare you speak about my Lord like that! I'll kill you!" Kayla yelled as she ran towards Alexander. The short knife in her hands suddenly began morphing into a long sword with a serrated edge. As she swung her sword towards Alexander, he deflected her attack. Alexander was about to launch a counter-attack, but in an instant, Kayla was gone. Alexander and Frieda stood back to back, thinking that Kayla could strike from any direction.

"Castellan won't stop until he retrieves Marissa's sword!" Yelled Kayla.

"Who the hell is Marissa?" Asked Alexander.

Kayla laughed. "Of course you don't know." She said, "just ask Heinrich."

Kayla suddenly appeared next to Alexander, and swung her sword at him. Alexander had only a split second to react. He blocked her attack, before she suddenly appeared behind Frieda. Before she could attack Frieda, however, Alexander forced her away with the Blade. Kayla appeared in front of Alexander, to which he deflected her attack. Kayla and Alexander swung back and forth at each other, while Kayla laughed hysterically.

"The pillars," Kayla said, "Their energy radiates from you, as it does from me."

"The... you know about the pillars?" Said Frieda.

"Of course I know about them!" Kayla said. "I found the pillars when I was just a child, and they gave me the power to make weapons from my hands. But their power comes with a consequence. For you, it's the constant pain."

Frieda stepped back with disbelief.

"I don't know what my consequence is though. " Said Kayla. "Castellan tells me it's my sanity, but I feel just fine!"

"When will you realize," said Alexander." Castellan is just a genocidal maniac. After you kill us, he'll just dispose of you like trash."

In Kayla's eyes, there was the fury of 100 sun's. "How dare you!" She yelled, running towards Alexander. As she got close, Alexander swung the Blade at her, which she backed away from, only to feel a horrible pain in her back. She looked behind her to see Frieda's threads wrapped around her. But instead of feeling mad, Kayla could only feel amazed by Frieda and Alexander's strategic genius. They had used her own insanity against her, luring her into a trap.

Kayla laid there on the floor. She looked over to see her legs and waist severed, a meter away. The look on her face changed from one of pure fury, to one of sorrow. Tears formed in her eyes.

"I'm sorry." She mumbled. "My mind has been restored. I'm so sorry."

"Bullshit!" Alexander yelled out.

"When someone is close to death, the Pillars will take back their power, and the consequences." Said Kayla. "Since I'm dying, the pillars have taken back my power, and restored my mind."

"There's no way that's true!" That Alexander.

"No, I believe her." Said Frieda, much to Alexanders supprise. "Since we met her, I could feel the Pillar's energy radiating off her, but its now gone."

Alexander looked at Frieda with disbelief, and then towards Kayla.

"Kayla, does Castellan have any weaknesses you know about?" Said Alexander.

"No, I'm sorry." Said Kayla. "I wish he did. I wish I had some way to help you, or any information I can give you. I'm sorry."

Kayla was clearly in horrible grief. In order to put her at ease, Alexander grabbed her hand.

"Promise me you'll kill that psychopathic bastard." She said.

"I promise." Alexander said. "I'll defeat him no matter what."

Kayla chuckled, and closed her eyes. Her palms became cold, and her breathing stopped. Alexander and Frieda were filled with grief. Kayla was an innocent woman, forced to the side of evil, and manipulated. Neither Alexander or Frieda could place the blame of what happened on her, even if they wanted to.

Minutes later, Heinrich woke up. He found himself wrapped in bandages, with Alexander and Frieda looking over him

"What happened?" Said Heinrich.

"Kayla betrayed us." Said Frieda.

"That lying bitch!" Exclaimed Heinrich, with a shocked look on his face.

"Don't call her that!" Snapped Frieda. "She was broken mentally, and used by Castellan. She never wanted any of this!"

"Is there any way you can bring her back?" Said Alexander. "Is there any spell or something to revive the dead?"

"No," Said Heinrich. "Death is almost irreversible. Only Time Control can undo it."

Frieda grabbed Alexander by the shirt and pushed him to a wall. "Bring her back!" She demanded. "You know how to use Time Control. You just haven't been trying hard enough. Bring her back!"

Alexander raised his hand towards Kayla's body, and put all his strength into trying to use Time Control, but to no avail. Just like always, the image of Erwins body flooded his mind, stopping his sorcery in its tracks. Frieda was devastated.

Alexander looked towards Heinrich. "Heinrich, who is Marissa?" He said.

"Kayla mentioned her, didn't she?" Said Heinrich.

"Who is Marissa?" Alexander repeated.

"As I told you when you first appeared in front of me those years ago, Castellan was once an ordinary man." Said Heinrich. "Like any other ordinary man, he had a wife, Marissa."

"Marissa was Castellan's wife?" Said Frieda with confusion.

"Yes." Said Heinrich. "Marissa was a warrior, the best in all of Deinceps."

"Kayla referred to the Blade Of Death as Marissa's Sword." Said Alexander. "Did you turn Marissa's sword into the Blade Of Death?"

"You're precisely right." Said Heinrich. "By the time the Blade was created, Castellan had already acquired his own Relic, meaning he could destroy it. To prevent this, we tried using a sword that we thought had sentimental value towards him."

"Castellan has a Relic?" Alexander said.

"Yes," said Heinrich, "it's a large scythe that allows him to teleport anywhere in the world, that's how he appeared in front of the Council building."

"I didn't see him use a Scythe then." Frieda said.

"Because he couldn't summon it." Heinrich said. "When he made it, he didn't infuse a normal scythe with sorcery, he instead did it with the black smoke he Simmons, that he simply shaped into a scythe. The Relic is stored as Energy in his body, which is why we couldn't take it away from him when we sealed him underground, and why he can use its abilities without materializing it."

"Did your plan to stop him from destroying the Blade work?" Asked Alexander.

"No," Said Heinrich. "Unfortunately, Castellan lost all his humanity, and all his morals. He was willing to destroy the Blade and kill Marissa as if they never meant anything to him."

"Oh my God, what the hell happened to him?" Said Frieda.

"Castellan was the first to discover Life Force." Explained Heinrich. "As soon as he discovered it, he began making ways to control it, steal it. Despite warnings from everyone around him, he developed Dark Sorcery. But Dark Sorcery didn't work how he intended it to. It took control over him, it took away everything that made him human."

Alexander looked out of the cave to see the sun, almost hidden behind the mountains. "It's getting late." He said. "We should rest for the night."

"Very well," said Heinrich. "It'd be dumb to move at night."

After extinguishing their fire, Heinrich quickly fell asleep. Alexander tried, but couldn't. Frieda didn't even bother trying. Alexander, seeing

Frieda standing by herself, decided to chat with her. "Are you alright?" Alexander asked Frieda.

"Just a few hours ago, we were trying to kill each other," she said, "Hell, I felt proud when I finally got her. Why do I mourn her now?"

"Because she's just like you." Said Alexander, to Frieda's confusion. "She's an innocent girl who was given powers she didn't want, and forced into fighting."

"Once we win," said Frieda, "I'll destroy the pillars. Nobody else will be given their curse, maybe it'll even rid the whole world of sorcery."

"We can do that once we defeat Castellan." Said Alexander. "But in order to do that, we must be well rested. Please get some sleep."

"You're right," said Frieda. "Goodnight."

Chapter Four: Rage

The next morning, the three woke up. They gathered their belongings, and left the cave. After a short while of walking, Alexander noticed strange markings on a tree, and they knew what it meant, they were in a bears territory. Alexander was rightfully worried, yet Frieda stayed confident as always. Their suspicions were soon proven correct, as a large Brown Bear suddenly got in the groups way, growling and standing on its hind legs. The group jumped back, and Alexander fell to the floor.

"Holy shit, that thing is massive!" Said Alexander.

"It's at least 2 and a half meters tall." Said Frieda, unraveling her fingernails to kill the bear.

"Slow down there," said Alexander. "You got that Giant yesterday, let me kill this bear."

Frieda chuckled. "Go ahead." She said, retracting her fingernails.

The bear swung its claws at Alexander, as he unsheathed the blade. And before the bear had time to react, Alexander appeared behind it, as its arm and head fell to the floor. Heinrich was very openly impressed, Frieda was also impressed, but tried to hide it. And so, the group continued on their journey. They soon passed through a large creek, and Heinrich seemed very happy to see this.

"Our destination is only a quarter of a kilometer away.' He said. Frieda and Alexander were excited to hear this, but also very anxious. But they didn't have time to gather themselves before the forest suddenly ended, and the village was in sight. As they entered the village, it was dead quiet.

"Is it normally this quiet?" Asked Frieda.

"Not usually," said Heinrich, "keep your guard up."

They walked past a couple houses, looking out for anything unusual. This village was usually packed with people, both residents and travelers. This sudden silence was very suspicious. And suddenly, there was a loud yelling behind them. They looked back to see a man running at them with a sword in his hands. His bad posture told them that he was no warrior, and his scared expression only proved this. Heinrich waved his hand, and the sword vanished.

"Please, no more!" The man pleaded.

"Listen, we're here to help you." Said Alexander. "Tell us what happened."

"I don't know anything about the Totem, no-one here does!" He yelled.

Frieda grabbed the man. "We're not here to hurt you, we're here to help. Please just tell us what happened." She said with a gentle voice. Alexander and Heinrich were surprised that she could talk so softly and calmly.

The man seemed to calm down. He was still afraid, but he could at least answer the questions now.

"Last night, a man appeared from no-where," he said, "there was a thunderstorm, and lightning struck in the middle of our village. A man appeared from the bolt."

The man's story reminded Alexander of Kayla. He slowly reached for the Blades handle, but didn't touch it

"He killed my friends and family right in front of me!" The man said. "He kept on asking about something called a Totem."

"Get out of the village," Heinrich said. "We'll take it from here."

The man thanked the group, and walked up. The ground began shaking violently. The ground around the edges of the village began tearing apart, as the village itself began shaking even more violently. Castellan's black smoke began rising from the cracks, as the group felt themselves rising. Alexander peeked over the edge to see that the entire village was rising from the ground. The black smoke got thicker, until it eventually let almost no light through. The man freaked out and tried running away, but when he touched the smoke, he suddenly caught fire, and died. Frieda looked at his corpse to see that the entire front side of his body had melted off, she almost threw up seeing this.

Alexander poked the Black smoke with the Blade. The tip of the Blade caught fire, but didn't melt like the man did, and the fire quickly dissipated. Alexander picked up a small rock and threw it into the smoke, it caught fire and melted.

"The smoke can destroy almost anything," he said, "but it looks like it still can't destroy Relics." Henrich was still shocked by this sudden predicament, yet was also impressed by Alexander's quick grasp of the situation and ability to gather information.

As the village reached 50 meters in the sky, it stopped ascending. The black smoke surrounding the village started shaking and rippling. A Husk suddenly appeared from the smoke and ran towards Heinrich, he quickly killed it. Everyone was shocked. More Husks quickly appeared from the smoke, and were killed even quicker. The speed at which they appeared slowly increased. The three stood back to back, covering all angles. Even with all angles covered, however, there were still too many Husks, the group was quickly overwhelmed.

Soon, a Husk manages to land a hit on Alexander, scarring his face. Upon seeing this, Heinrich levitated the three to different rooftops, out of the Husks reach. Frieda and Heinrich panicked, and Alexander collapsed on the floor, crying.

"Each and every one of those Husks used to be a person," he said, "an innocent man woman or child who never did anything to deserve this. There are hundreds, several villages worth of innocent people, practically killed."

All the Husks suddenly stopped. One of them climbed on the roof Alexander was standing on. Alexander looked up at it. Even with its distorted and disfigured face, he could recognize it, it was the Husk that was once Erwin. Upon seeing it, Alexander jumped up, dropped the Blade, and hugged it.

"I'm so sorry!" He sobbed. "It's all my fault! It's my fault you died and got revived as this monster!"

The Husk jabbed it's sharp nails into Alexander's sides. Alexander cried out in pain, but didn't loosen his grip.

"I know this isn't you." Alexander said. "Please, free yourself from Castellan, regain yourself."

The Husk didn't care what Alexander was saying. It winded back its arm, preparing to strike Alexander and kill him. Alexander continued sobbing and pleading with the Husk, but it didn't listen. Right as it was about to kill Alexander, he grabbed the Blade and stabbed it through the chest. As the Husk's body fell to the floor, tears dripped down Alexander's face.

"I'm sorry." He muttered. "I'm so fucking sorry."

The other Husks started moving again. They climbed up the building, completely surrounding Alexander. Alexander's sadness, however, quickly turned to rage. With one swing of the Blade, the Husks surrounding him all fell to the floor, lifeless. In his rage, Alexander jumped onto the ground in the swarm of Husks, killing several at a time with each swing of the Blade. Heinrich prepared to jump down to help him, but Frieda grabbed him by the arm and pulled him back.

"You need to save your Life Energy to make that Lantern, remember? She said, "Let me do this."

Heinrich chuckled and stepped back. Frieda quickly jumped off the roof and joined the fight. Alexander's rampage had made the swarm of Husks much less dense than before, giving Frieda a clear window to join the fight. Upon hitting the ground, some Husks quickly began charging her. Frieda's long range and flexibility, however, made it easy for her to cover all angles. With quick swings of her arms, Frieda could kill several Husks at once. Alexander didn't even seem to notice her in the fight, as he was completely blinded by rage. His screams of anger and grief could be heard from the ground.

Alexander continued his rampage. Eventually, as he swung the Blade, there was a loud pop sound. Heinrich recognized this as the same one from when Alexander was trying to retrieve the Blade during his fight with Castellan. In his rage, Alexander was completely oblivious to the fact that his injuries were getting worse. The Husks started appearing slower, and everyone knew what this meant. Castellan was running out of them. They all suddenly stopped, and retreated back into the smoke walls. With the Husks gone, Alexander's rage ended. All the pain he couldn't feel before suddenly rushed back into him, causing him to fall to his knees.

Frieda ran towards him. He was bleeding heavily from his sides, and his legs were splintering because they hadn't fully healed from before. Frieda reached into her pocket to grab a bandage, but she didn't have any. She had used all of them to treat Heinrich's wounds from when Kayla attacked. Frieda took off her jacket, and tore off part of it, using that as a makeshift bandage. Heinrich was preparing a healing spell, when there was a sudden rumble. The smoke wall began shaking violently, and rippling. Everyone knew something big was trying to come through. Alexander tried standing up to fight, but couldn't.

His attempt to stand up causes more blood to leave his body, seeping through his makeshift bandage. His skin suddenly became a little more pale, and suddenly felt very high. He grabbed Frieda by the arm with his little strength.

"Your eyes are beautiful." He muttered, seemingly unaware of the situation. Frieda didn't even seem to notice what he said, as she started dragging him to an abandoned building for safety.

"Please, won't you dance with me?" Alexander said as Frieda left him behind in the cover. Frieda faintly smiled hearing this, but the smile quickly faded.

"Heinrich!" Frieda yelled. "Treat Alexander's wounds, I'll deal with whatever is coming out of that wall."

"Are you sure you can handle it?" Heinrich asked.

"Why do you always underestimate me?" Frieda said with an offended tone. "Alexander is currently out of commission, and you need to save your Life Energy. That only leaves me to fight."

Chapter Six: Blaze

The ground began shaking again, as a giant horn appeared from the wall. Frieda climbed on a building and prepared to fight whatever was coming. There was a loud roar from the smoke wall, and the shaking got worse. The head of the beast fully emerged. Frieda looked up at it in horror, this beast was a large dragon. Frieda unraveled her threads and attempted to kill the dragon, only for the threads to bounce off its impenetrable scales. The dragon opened its mouth, and a bright light appeared from its throat.

Frieda quickly jumped off the roof, and tried to get out of the dragon's sight. The entire village was heated up, as the dragon blew a large ball of fire towards the buildings. Shrapnel was launched across the whole village. Frieda looked over at the building Heinrich and Alexander were in. Alexander was unconscious, and Heinrich was completely focused on saving him. Frieda wanted to devise a plan with Heinrich, but she knew he couldn't take his focus away from Alexander. And besides, her going there would draw the dragons attention towards Heinrich and Alexander.

The smoke wall began rippling again, and more of the dragon appeared. Now, its entire neck was out. Frieda was amazed, yet terrified of the dragon's size. Its neck alone was 15 meters across, and its entire body probably couldn't fit inside the village. Frieda left her cover and ran back towards the Dragon. The Dragon, seeing her, launched another fireball towards her. Frieda dodged it, but was hit by a piece of shrapnel in her leg. The shockwave of the explosion threw her off the building.

Despite Frieda's wounds and the hopelessness of her situation, her fighting spirit remained strong.

The dragon, assuming Frieda had been killed, continued trying to emerge from the smoke wall. A thread suddenly wrapped around one of its horns. The dragon looked down to see Frieda carrying herself towards it. She had wrapped her thread around the Dragons horn, and was retracting it to bring herself towards the Dragon. The Dragon tried to launch another fireball, but by the time the fireball was charged up, Frieda had already leveled with the Dragon, and her momentum carried her up even further.

There's no scales on its eyes, Frieda thought to herself. *The eyes must be its weak points.* Frieda launched her threads towards the dragon's eyes, the threads bounced off. Despite the lack of scales, the eyes were still too tough for the threads to cut through. The Dragon launched the fireball it had already charged up at Frieda, and with her suspended in the air, she couldn't dodge it. Right before the fireball hit her, there was a bright purple flash, and the fireball froze in place. Frieda looked down to see that Heinrich had done this using his Sorcery. He swung his arm in the direction of the Dragon, and the fireball launched back towards it, stunning it for just a second. Heinrich used his sorcery to safely bring Frieda back down towards him.

"What the hell are you doing?" Frieda yelled. "You need to conserve your Life Energy, remember?"

"It's okay," Heinrich said, "I have plenty.

"Well you still need to treat Alexander's wounds." Frieda said.

"That's already done." Heinrich said.

"Then where is he?" Frieda said.

"He's hidden away in a building," Heinrich said, "Although his wounds are healed, he's still far too weak to fight."

There was a loud roar, the Dragon had regained itself, and it was pissed off.

"We'll discuss this later." Heinrich said, preparing to fight. He filled one hand with a purple energy, and the other with a blue energy. He then quickly dropped them to the floor. The two energies dispersed across the island. Frieda lost her balance as the floating village violently shook. Two large creatures appeared from the ground, to Frieda's amazement. The creatures looked like dragon's, but were made entirely out of the stone from the ground. They were large, about twice the size of the actual dragon's head. The stone golem's quickly ran towards the actual dragon, biting it in the head and neck, the dragon wasn't hurt at all.

"Those stone golem's have a bite force 100 times that of a bear, and the dragon still isn't hurt?" Heinrich said.

"My threads didn't do shit either." Said Frieda.

"If we can't even pierce it's skin," Heinrich said, "that means the Blade is completely useless against it."

The Dragon managed to knock away the two stone golem's.

"Heinrich, retreat with Alexander." Frieda said. "If you die, we can't make the Mystic Veil. If I die, it means nothing."

"Hell no," said Heinrich. "I refuse to abandon you here, even if it costs me my life."

Before they could say anything else, the Dragon launched a fireball at them. The fireball came without warning, so they didn't have time to run away, and casting a shield would also take too long. Heinrich pushed Frieda away with a spell, catching the fireball head-on. Instead of the fire dispersing out, it all was absorbed by Heinrich, yet he wasn't burned at all. Frieda looked at Heinrich in horror.

"D-did you just absorb the fireball?" She muttered. "Absorbed your enemies attack is a form of Dark Sorcery."

Heinrich looked at Frieda in shame. "Frieda, I can explain." He said. Heinrich took a step towards Frieda, to which Frieda swung her threads at him. The threads didn't kill Heinrich, but they did scar his face.

"Stay away from me!" Frieda yelled in terror, backing away from Heinrich. "So that's how you've been able to recover from your injuries so fast, by stealing Life Energy from other living beings!"

"I promise, I only ever used it on plants," Heinrich said, "and I swear I haven't let it corrupt my soul like it did to Castellan."

"Time Control, the Mystic Veil, and now Dark Sorcery," Frieda said, "How many more things are you hiding from us?"

The Dragon launched another fireball at them. Heinrich raised one hand to cast a shield without even facing the Dragon, completely blocking the fireball. The stone golem's forced their way back onto the Dragon, keeping it occupied for a little bit longer. There was a sudden noise from a building. Frieda and Heinrich looked over to see Alexander stumbling out, using the Blade as a walking stick because he was still too weak to walk upright. He was shocked seeing how tense Frieda and Heinrich were at each other.

"What the hell happened here?" He said.

"Alexander, stay back." Frieda said. "Heinrich has been using Dark Sorcery."

"No," Alexander muttered, "that's impossible. You wouldn't do that, right, Heinrich."

The look of shame on Heinrich's face confirmed it for Alexander.

"How could you do this?" Alexander said. "You know the consequences of using Dark Sorcery better than anyone else. You've witnessed firsthand what it does, why would you use it?"

"Will you both please just shut the hell up!" Heinrich snapped. Frieda and Alexander were shocked by this sudden outburst. "I know how you feel, I understand your concerns, but I promise I am never going to turn out like Castellan. I would never use this power for evil, and I refuse to let it corrupt my soul!"

"I don't know if I can trust you anymore." Frieda said with a heartbroken tone in her voice.

"Frieda please," Heinrich said, "this is the worst possible time for something to come between us. If we fall apart now, we die!"

Alexander walked towards Heinrich, and put his hand on his shoulder.

"No matter what, I trust you." He said. Frieda felt betrayed by Alexander siding with Heinrich over her, but Heinrich was relieved. The Dragon once again pushed away the stone golem's. This time, it bit off their heads, killing both of them.

"Frieda, will you fight with me?" Heinrich said. "All three of our lives are on the line, we can argue later. Please, fight with me."

Frieda stood still with a shocked expression on her face. Heinrich knew that she wouldn't fight. Alexander tried fully standing up, but fell over.

"You aren't fully healed yet." Heinrich said, "stay out of this for now, and leave it to me."

The dragon launched a fireball at Heinrich, which he blocked with a shield. Heinrich levitated till he was eye level with the Dragon. The Dragon, realizing that its fireballs were pointless, forced more of its body out from the smoke wall. The Dragon extended its neck and tried biting Heinrich, but Heinrich suddenly teleported behind it. Heinrich spread out his arms, and two dark clouds appeared in the palms of his hands. The clouds slowly grew large, covering his entire arms, and connecting at his chest. Heinrich quickly snapped his hands together, as the clouds began glowing purple.

"This is one of my strongest spells," he said, "witness pure destructive energy!"

A purple bolt of lightning shot from Heinrichs arms and hit the Dragon. The Dragon yelled in pain, and started lightly bleeding from the point of impact. Alexander noticed this wound, and realized what he needed to do. That wound was the only place where he could use the Blade on the Dragon, but he was still too weak to fight.

"Heinrich, get over here!" Alexander yelled. Heinrich quickly flew over towards him.

"I have a plan to kill the Dragon, but I need your help." He said. "Levitate me over towards the Dragon so I can hit that wound with the Blade."

"I'm sorry, but I don't think I have the energy." Heinrich said, exhausted. "I could probably levitate you over there, but I don't think you have the strength to deal that blow on it."

The Dragon stood there, watching them. It knew not to launch a fireball, as Heinrich could absorb it.

"Then what the hell are we supposed to do?" Alexander said.

"Heinrich," Frieda muttered, "you made the Blade, right?"

"Yes, where are you going with this?" Heinrich responded.

"Then you should be able to reprogram it," She said, "take away its locking mechanism, then I can use it."

"That's not possible." Heinrich said. "A Relic cannot have its programming changed, all I can do is delay its effects."

Frieda stepped back in shock, contemplating her next move. "Once you kill Castellan, do me a favor and destroy those pillars." She said,

Frieda ran past Alexander, and snatched the Blade from his hands. Frieda felt a shock run through her body, but he didn't die. She looked over to see Heinrich using his sorcery to delay the Blades locking mechanism. Frieda wrapped her threads around a street light, and used it to launch herself upwards, in her threads range of the Dragon. She then wrapped her threads around one of the Dragons horns, and pulled herself within arms length of the wound.

Frieda stood on the Dragon's neck, and grasped the Blade in both hands, pointed it down. She raised the Blade into the air, and quickly dragged it down into the wound. As the Blade entered the Dragon's body, it raged. The Dragon spewed straight fire from its mouth, hollering so loud it shook the whole village. Its violent shaking threw Frieda off its neck, to which she used her Threads to guide herself towards Heinrich and Alexander. Heinrich was in pain, as he was straining his own Life Energy to keep Frieda alive, but alas, he lost the strength to keep the spell going.

As the Spell stopped, Frieda felt another great shock, ten times greater than the one before.

"Frieda!" Alexander yelled with pain in his voice.

"So this is it," Frieda said, "this is how I die.

"No!" Alexander yelled. "you aren't gonna die! You're stronger than this! We need you!"

Frieda wrapped her arm around the back of Alexander's head, as he fought to hold back tears.

"Alexander, listen," Frieda said, "The pain, it's gone."

Alexander's eyes widened in shock. Frieda stretched out her hand, and nothing happened.

"My powers don't work either." She muttered. Alexander yelled in horror. Her skin slowly became more pale, and her voice softened.

"You're strong." Frieda muttered softly. "You alone hold the strength to defeat Castellan, don't waste your one chance mourning over me."

Alexander's head lowered, as he sobbed uncontrollably. Frieda looked over at Heinrich, who was struggling to compose himself.

"I'm sorry." She said, "You brought me in when I was at my lowest, you were just like a father to me. I'm so sorry I freaked out at you, I'm so sorry I hurt you."

"It's okay, I forgive you," Heinrich said, "I betrayed your trust, you had every right to be mad at me."

Frieda looked back at Alexander, who's sobbing had turned into full crying. Frieda was feeling a flurry of emotions like fear and grief, but she knew which one to let take over for her last moments. Frieda wrapped her other arm around his head, and pulled him down, kissing him. Alexander's crying stopped for a moment.

"Hey, dumbass," She muttered softly, "promise me you'll keep moving forward, and some time in the far future, me and you can meet again in the afterlife."

Alexander struggled to not break out crying again. "I promise I'll fight till the end!" He said. A light smile appeared on Frieda's face hearing this, as she let go of Alexander.

"Frieda, no!" Alexander yelled, knowing why she had let go of him. He tried grabbing her hand, but she didn't grip it. Alexander fell to the floor, uncontrollably crying. Heinrich finally failed to compose himself, as he too let himself shed tears.

"Goddammit!" Heinrich sobbed. Alexander grabbed the Blade off the floor where Frieda had set it down.

"Damn you, you worthless piece of shit!" Alexander said, "This is all your fault!"

Alexander, in his rage, punched the flat end of the Blade. Though he was trying to make it seem like he was mad at the Blade, Heinrich could tell that Alexander was truly mad at himself. Alexander was mad because he believed Frieda would still be alive, had it not been for his own lack of strength. The village started shaking violently. The duo's mourning was temporarily overtaken by the fear of what was to come. After the army of Husks and the Dragon, they didn't know if they'd have the strength to defeat whatever was next. The earth below them shattered. Giant cracks appeared on the floor, all appearing to come from the same spot.

The smoke wall surrounding the village faded away, as the entire village was reduced to mere rubble. Just as the footing below him crumbled, Heinrich launched himself towards Alexander to cast a shield for both of them. The two looked at the source of this destruction, to see a large metal ball attached to a chain. It appeared to have torn through the ground from below, and its momentum continued raising it into the air. The metal ball suddenly stopped, and was ripped back down. This created a second impact that scattered the rubble of the village.

As they hit the ground, the shield vanished. Heinrich was exhausted, but Alexander was still unharmed. Heinrich looked terrified, as if he knew what was happening. Alexander was confused for only a second, before realizing it himself. This destruction was caused by the Husk of Thomas.

"Alexander," Heinrich said, "I don't have enough Life Energy to cast any spells, at least not any spells that can hurt Thomas."

"What are you implying?" Asked Alexander.

"I'm going to give you some of mine." Said Heinrich. "Don't worry, I'll still keep enough for me to survive, but not enough to aid you at all. In the meantime, I'll try stealing some Life Energy from surrounding plants, but I still doubt I'll have enough to cast any spells."

A boulder near them shattered, it seemed like Thomas was looking for them.

"Heinrich, that's a horrible idea!" Alexander said. "Let's fight together." Alexander tried standing, but immediately fell over.

"Right now you're too weak to stand, let alone fight." Heinrich said. "Trust me, this is the only way we can win."

The look of horror on Alexander's face slowly turned to a look of trust, and Heinrich took that as a sign to proceed. There was a bright white light, as Heinrich gave his Life Energy to Alexander. Heinrich fell to the floor, too pathetic to even crawl. However, Alexander suddenly felt more powerful than ever before. The bright flash gave away their position to Thomas, who almost instantly attacked. Alexander quickly dodged, and carried Heinrich to safety.

Chapter Seven: Goodbye

"Well, if it isn't my old student." Thomas said seeing Alexander approach him.

"Well, if it isn't a puppet that looks like my old master, controlled by a man too cowardly to face me himself." Alexander said.

Thomas' Husk laughed. "Throughout the years, I've been improving my Husk conversion spells." It said, "Now, I can make a husk look almost identical to its original human, along with keeping its physical attributes."

"I'll grant you this one monologue for fun, but I won't be so generous the next time." Alexander said.

Thomas's Husk laughed even more. "I appreciate your generosity. Well just a month ago, I finally mastered the art." It said. "I can make a Husk completely identical to a human, with all its same strengths and weaknesses! Now, Husks can even use Relics and possibly sorcery."

"And what's your point?" Alexander said.

"I was planning on turning Kayla into a Husk," it said, "but you did me the liberty of killing her before I could, but It's no problem, she was already so insane that she mindlessly followed every order from me."

Alexander seemed frustrated at this statement, but kept his composure.

"Now that I think about it," the Husk said, "you and Heinrich would make fine Husks."

Alexander chuckled. "You can certainly try to convert us."

"That girl would've also made a great Husk, too bad *you* killed-"

Before the Husk could finish its sentence, Alexander was right in front of it, with the Blade mere inches from its face, Thomas just barely managed to dodge it. Thomas quickly backed away from Alexander, only for Alexander to appear behind him. Alexander was much closer this time, so Thomas knew he couldn't dodge. Instead, Thomas hit his flail against the ground, creating a shockwave that knocked Alexander back.

There were now several meters between the two. Thomas swept his flail over the ground, which Alexander dodged by jumping over. Alexander instantly closed the gap between them, and swung the sword down at Thomas. Thomas dodged, and grabbed Alexander by the hands, trying to prevent him from using the Blade. Alexander managed to flick the sword at Thomas, forcing him away. Thomas quickly created distance, and launched his Flail at Alexander. Alexander held his sword at an angle to push him away, the same maneuver he used against Castellan. As the Flail hit the Blade, there was a giant shockwave that knocked both Alexander and Thomas off their feet.

Alexander got back up, but noticed something off with the Blade, its edge was chipped. Thomas laughed realizing this.

"Do you remember nothing from your training?" Thomas said, "Nothing can damage a Relic, other than another Relic. You must've gotten so use to your Blade being indestructible, you act recklessly with it. I'm the first threat you've faced that can shatter your Blade, and you'll be helpless to stop me after that."

Thomas threw another attack at Alexander. Alexander, realizing he couldn't deflect the attack, quickly dodged it. Alexander quickly began closing the distance between him and Thomas. Thomas swept his flail across the ground again, which Alexander jumped over. As Alexander reached Thomas, he attempted to swing the Blade at him, which Thomas dodged, before punching Alexander in the stomach. Alexander was knocked back for a moment, before launching another attack at Thomas. Thomas tried hitting Alexander with his flail in an attempt to force Alexander to back away, but Alexander managed to dodge without extending the gap at all. Thomas threw another attack, which Alexander once again dodged without backing away. In one final attempt to back Alexander away, Thomas quickly spun around, launching the flail in all directions. Just like before, Alexander quickly backed away. The flail suddenly appeared right in front of him. Alexander, not having time to dodge, was forced to block it with the Blade.

Alexander looked at the Blade. The Blade wasn't yet shattered, but there was a large crack going straight through it, and the edge was even further chipped. He felt exhausted, but had to keep fighting on. Alexander stood up, but quietly fell to the floor in pain. Alexander coughed into his hand, and was shocked to see blood there. Thomas, seeing this, laughed.

"You are pathetic." He said. "You cannot defeat me."

Alexander mustered the strength to stand, and ran towards Thomas. He tried hitting him with the Blade, Thomas easily dodged it and punched Alexander in the stomach again.

"The girl is already dead, and both you and Heinrich are far too weak to defeat me." Thomas said. Alexander stood back up, and tried attacking Thomas. Thomas dodged, and punched Alexander in the wrists, causing him to drop the Blade. Thomas hit Alexander with an uppercut to the chin, knocking him away. Alexander tried standing up again, but couldn't, as he was too injured.

"Once I kill you and shattered the Blade," said Thomas, "none shall stand in my way." Thomas grabbed Alexander by the hair, and wound back the flail to hit him with it. A pair of hands suddenly grabbed Thomas by the head, and Thomas began feeling tired. He quickly swung the flail back to see Heinrich. Heinrich quickly used a spell to push himself back away from the flail. Heinrich used another spell to push Thomas back, before running towards Alexander.

"Alexander, are you alright?" Heinrich said.

"I'm fine," Alexander said, attempting to stand up again, and falling back down. "How are you back up already?"

"With Dark Sorcery," said Heinrich, "I absorbed Life Energy from the grass, just enough to get back on my feet. I snuck up behind Thomas, and absorbed some of his life energy as well."

Heinrich located Alexander's wounds, and hovered his hands over them. A soft yellow light was emitted from his hands, and Alexander suddenly felt his wounds healing.

"So the rumors are true," said Thomas, "the mighty Heinrich has been using Dark Sorcery. Are you not afraid you might end up like me?"

"I'll never be like you." Heinrich said.

Thomas launched the flail towards Heinrich, who quickly dodged it by falling to the floor. Heinrich gathered a purple energy in his hands, before slamming it into the ground. Thomas found himself unable to stand, as the ground beneath him turned to sand. Alexander took advantage of this, and attempted to stab Thomas with the Blade. Thomas tried attacking Alexander with the flail, but was off balance, so Alexander easily dodged it. Alexander was about to stab Thomas, before Thomas managed to crawl out of the sand pit to dodge it. The sand pit began glowing purple, before violently erupting, creating a cloud of dust that blinded him.

The cloud only lasted for a second before fading away, but in that second, Thomas saw a sudden silver light surrounding him. As the cloud cleared away, Thomas found himself completely surrounded by what appeared to be clones of Alexander. The clones quickly began charging towards Thomas, who spun his flail around to launch it in all directions. As it hit the clones, they disappeared into a silver light. These were not physical clones, but merely illusions casted by Heinrich. As the illusions disappeared, Thomas couldn't see Alexander or Heinrich, they were hiding somewhere.

THE GROUND SUDDENLY began glowing purple and blue, and a stone golem appeared from it. Thomas launched his Flail at it, killing it instantly. A second stone golem appeared, and caught the flail in its mouth, before yanking on it to try to pull it out of Heinrich's hands. Thomas managed to keep a grip on the Flail, but couldn't pull it away from the stone golem. A silver light appeared next to Thomas, and Alexander emerged with the Blade. Thomas believed this was another illusion, before noticing the dirt displace below its feet, this was the real one. Thomas tried attacking him with the flail, but couldn't, as the stone golem kept a grip on it. Seeing the Blade grow closer to him, Thomas finally let go of the flail to dodge Alexander's attack.

The stone golem, finally having control over the flail, tossed it to the ground, before falling apart into a pile of rubble. Another silver light appeared, and Heinrich emerged from it. Heinrich grabbed the flail, before both him and the flail began glowing white. The flail's light suddenly grew dimmer, as Heinrich's light grew brighter. As the Flail light completely died out, Heinrich dropped it, before he also stopped glowing. Thomas watched in horror, and quickly ran to grab the flail. It was harder to swing than before, the chain couldn't grow anymore, and it didn't hit as hard.

"What the hell did you do?" Yelled Thomas.

Dark clouds began forming around Heinrich's arms. Thomas, knowing what was happening, began running away. As the clouds started glowing purple, Heinrich clapped his hands together. A purple bolt of lighting was shot out towards Thomas. Thomas tried to dodge it, but the lighting was drawn towards him.

"As powerful as you may be," Thomas muttered, "only one of us will be left standing in the end, and it definitely won't be you."

The lighting bolt hit Thomas, as he screamed in pain. Only a second later, Thomas was vaporized into a red mist. Heinrich fell to the floor, exhausted. Alexander looked at the mist in terror.

"What did you do?" Said Alexander.

"Pure Destructive Energy," said Heinrich, "the same spell I used on the Dragon."

"And what happened to the Flail?" Said Alexander.

"I absorbed the Life Energy in it, turning it from a Relic into an ordinary object."

Heinrich looked towards a nearby cave, and stood up. "That's where the Totem is." He said, pointing towards the cave. Alexander and Heinrich walked towards the cave. Inside, it looked completely normal, which confused Alexander.

"So, where is it?" Asked Alexander.

"Stand back." Said Heinrich. Heinrich suddenly gathered energy of all different colors in his hands, and launched it towards the back wall of the cave. The walls of the cave began glowing in Runes. Tiny glowing particles started appearing in the air, and suddenly grouped together in the middle of the cave. As the particles grouped together, the cluster of them started glowing brighter, as well as the Runes surrounding them. There was a powerful shockwave that pushed both Alexander and Heinrich off their feet, and everything stopped glowing.

Alexander stood up to see a glowing blue orb in the middle of the cave, suspended in the air. This was the Totem.

"What just happened?" Said Alexander.

"That was my way of preventing anyone else from getting the Totem." Heinrich said. "The Totem was being kept in a state of both existence and non-existence simultaneously. Only my Omnipotence could truly bring it into existence. Castellan knew this, which is why he didn't kill me while you were fighting Thomas."

Heinrich gathered a gold energy in his hands, and shaped it into an orb. He reached into the orb, and pulled out a lantern.

"Sit down and rest," Heinrich said, "I will begin work on the Mystic Veil."

Heinrich hit the Totem with a blue energy, the cave instantly filled with Runes. Alexander watched in awe as Heinrich changed the Runes, erased and adding new ones. He gathered Runes together in certain areas, making individual spells. After what felt like hours, Alexander peaked out of the cave to see the sun already setting.

"How much longer will this take?" Asked Alexander.

"I'm almost finished." Said Heinrich. "The creation of Relics is extremely difficult. There are thousands of Runes in a single Relic, and if even a single one is out of place, the whole Relic can be completely destroyed, taking the Totem with it."

After a few minutes, Alexander heard a noise outside of the cave. He peaked out to see a Husk, only a few meters away from them. Castellan must have sent out Husks to find them, knowing his plan to kill them had failed. Alexander told this to Heinrich, who didn't seem surprised.

"Prepare yourself," Heinrich said, "because every Husk in a kilometers radius is about to know our position."

Alexander seemed shocked to hear this.

"Cover your eyes." Heinrich said, Alexander immediately complied. The Totem and lantern began touching, and suddenly began fusing together. A bright light was emitted, creating a beacon that could be seen from a kilometer away. This light only lasted for a couple of seconds, before dying out. Alexander uncovered his eyes to see the Totem gone, and the lantern looking slightly different.

"What happened?" Said Alexander.

"It's finished." Said Heinrich. "This is it, the Mystic Veil, the key to our victory. All that's left to do is to find Castellan, and kill him."

A Husk entered the cave. It immediately charged towards Alexander. Heinrich held up the Mystic Veil, a bright light filled the room, and the Husk fell to the floor lifeless.

"I probably should have asked this earlier," said Alexander, "but if the Blade can no longer effect Castellan at all, then how exactly will the Mystic Veil help us win?"

"The Veil should weaken Castellan enough for the Blade to serve its original purpose." Said Heinrich. "Follow me."

Heinrich and Alexander exited the cave, only to find themselves surrounded by Husks. Alexander prepared himself to kill them all.

"Leave one alive." Said Heinrich. Alexander was confused, but followed his orders. Alexander effortlessly killed all but one of the Husks. Heinrich gathered a purple energy in his hands, and walked towards the remaining Husk. He placed his hands on the Husks shoulders, and its arms blew off. Heinrich then grabbed the helpless Husk by its neck.

"Castellan, I know you're watching." He said. "You know exactly where we are, and we've already proven that these Husks pose no threat to us. Your only possible way of defeating us now is to come fight us yourself instead of sending someone else."

Heinrich killed the Husk, as a dark cloud appeared in the sky. The sky dimmed, as the cloud swirled above them. A bolt of lighting struck in front of them, and there stood Castellan. Alexander stared in horror, before getting into a battle stance. Castellan noticed the Veil in Heinrich's hands.

"So that's what you used the Totem for." He said. "What does it do?"

"It ensures our victory." Heinrich said.

Castellan laughed. "How is Dark Sorcery treating you?" He said.

"Obviously much better than it treated you." He said to Castellan's amusement. "Though I'm not as powerful as you are, my soul has stayed pure."

Chapter Eight: Oh, how I've missed you all!

Without another word, Castellan charged towards Alexander. He moved so fast Alexander couldn't even see him coming, and almost hit him with his scythe. Heinrich immediately raised the Veil in the air. Castellan felt a shock throughout his entire body as the light hit him, and froze for just a second. In that second, Alexander tried to hit him with the Blade. Castellan backed away to dodge the attack. Alexander charged towards Castellan, and swung the Blade at him. Castellan blocked the attack with his Scythe, and attempted to launch a counter-attack. He suddenly felt a great pain throughout his body, and felt it more difficult to move. Castellan looked back to see Heinrich with both of his hands on his back, filling his body with a purple energy.

Castellan created a tentacle from his back, and attempted to kill Heinrich with it. With his powers nullified, the tentacle moved slow enough for Heinrich to dodge. Alexander attempted to attack Castellan again, only for him to block the attack. Castellan pushed the Blade away from himself, and tried hitting Alexander with his scythe. Alexander dodged, and backed away towards Heinrich.

"Be careful." Said Heinrich. "Though he can only use a tenth of his original power right now, he still has the strength to kill us in one hit."

Castellan noticed the Veil, suspended in mid-air, surrounded by a yellow energy. He began rushing towards it, attempting to destroy it. Heinrich gathered a purple and blue energy in his hands, and slammed them into the floor. The ground rumbled, and a stone golem appeared right below him, catching half of his body in its mouth. Castellan slammed his fist against the stone golem, attempting to make it drop him. Despite its face starting to crack, the stone golem refused to let go. Alexander quickly climbed it, attempting to attack Castellan with the Blade. Castellan, realizing he couldn't block the attack because he had dropped his Scythe, let out another attack. He quickly created tentacles across his entire body, and shot them out in all directions. The stone golem was killed, and Alexander was forced back.

Castellan fell to the ground, and immediately grabbed his scythe. A second stone golem appeared, and attempted to catch Castellan. Castellan instantly stabbed it in its face with the scythe, killing it. The ground filled with purple and yellow energy, as metal chains zipped up from the ground, and wrapped around Castellan. Alexander attempted to kill him again, assuming the chains could successfully restrain him. The chains, however, failed to restrain Castellan, as he managed to break them apart and forced Alexander back. The area suddenly filled with silver light, as Heinrich created hundreds of illusions that looked identical to the Veil. Castellan couldn't destroy the Veil, as he had no idea which one was the real one, and which ones were just illusions.

More chains appeared from the ground, and wrapped around Castellan's scythe, preventing him from using it. Alexander attempted to attack Castellan in the second it would take him to break the chains, but Castellan broke the chains much quicker than Alexander expected, forcing him back. Castellan suddenly lost his balance, as the ground beneath him turned to sand. The ground filled with purple energy, as the sand pit exploded into a cloud that blinded Castellan. When it cleared out, Castellan saw himself completely surrounded by illusions of Alexander, all charging towards him.

Castellan launched another omni-directional tentacle attack, destroying all of the illusions. As the tentacles disappeared, the real Alexander appeared in front of him, as well as Heinrich who was holding onto a purple energy.

In his weakened state, there's no way he can use that attack twice in less than a second Alexander thought to himself. To both Alexander and Heinrich's surprise, Castellan did manage to use that attack again, although he seemed tired. Heinrich and Alexander dodged the attack, but were temporarily off balance. At that moment, Castellan attempted to kill Heinrich with his scythe. Heinrich casted a shield just in time to not get stabbed, but most of the attacks force still hit him in the head, making him unable to use sorcery for a brief period of time. The illusions of the Mystic Veil disappeared, revealing the real one.

Castellan let out a smirk seeing this, and began marching towards the Veil. Alexander rushed in to try to stop him, but couldn't do anything, as Castellan easily overpowered him. Once Castellan reached the Veil, he lifted his Scythe into the air, and smashed it into the Veil, destroying it. A shockwave was released so powerful that it knocked Alexander off his feet. Castellan laughed hysterically, as all of his power returned to him. Alexander rushed towards Heinrich for guidance.

"What do we do now?" Asked Alexander.

"There's one last thing I've been hiding." Said Heinrich. "There's a spell I have that could potentially kill Castellan."

Alexander was shocked to hear this, Castellan decided to let Alexander and Heinrich have this moment out of courtesy.

"It's an extremely complicated power," said Heinrich, "Life Energy is not a physical thing, but with Black Energy, I can materialize it, forcing it to pretend to be physical. Anything this pretend mass comes into contact with will also get this pretend mass property, so when I let the spell go, anything it touches will be erased from existence."

"And why did you keep this a secret from us?" Alexander said.

"Because using it would kill me." Said Heinrich. "This pretend mass appears in a sphere around me, so I'm forced to be inside it, thus I will also be erased. I refused to use it because I was selfish, I valued my life over Castellan's death. But now I realize, Castellan's death is hundreds of times more important than my life."

"No," mumbled Alexander. "That's not selfishness, that's self preservation. If it wasn't for you, we never would've gotten this far without you. And it wouldn't be right for you to sacrifice yourself just to kill Castellan. Let's fight together."

"Alexander," said Heinrich, "We have to keep moving forward in life. We have to look towards the future, not the past. Time will keep moving on no matter what. So if we look towards the future, we will be prepared for whatever happens. But if we look towards the past, Time will move on without us, leaving us stranded in an unfamiliar world. Do you understand?"

Alexander was surprised to hear this, and terrified of its implications. "Yes, I understand." He said.

Heinrich chuckled. "That's good. When this is all over, I declare you the new leader of the Council, I'm entrusting its rebuild to you." He said. "We'll meet again in the afterlife one day, me you and Frieda."

Alexander froze in fear. Alexander suddenly found himself surrounded by a yellow energy, as Heinrich forced him back using his sorcery. Alexander tried to rush towards Heinrich, but couldn't.

"You don't have to do this!" He yelled. "Please, come back!" Tears dripped down his face, as he failed to compose himself any further. Heinrich ran towards Castellan, surrounded by a black energy. Heinrich fired another Pure Destructive in the hopes that it would do something and he wouldn't have to carry out with his current plan, but Castellan was completely unphased, simply laughing as the attack passed through him and did absolutely nothing. Suddenly, a Giant spherical formation of black crystals appeared around Him, completely engulfing him and Castellan. The yellow energy disappeared, and Alexander ran towards the sphere. Right before he touched it, it vanished into dust. Heinrich, Castellan, and the surrounding area completely vanished. Alexander fell to the floor, sobbing.

A black smoke suddenly appeared right where Castellan stood. Alexander watched in horror as the smoke grew in size, and shaped itself into Castellan.

"That was amazing." Said Castellan. "Complete erasure from existence, I'm surprised even I could survive that."

Alexander quickly grabbed the Blade, and ran toward Castellan. Alexander stabbed him straight through the stomach, the tip of the Blade poked out through his back. Castellan was completely unphased by this, simply laughing at Alexander's pathetic attempt at victory.

"With that Lantern gone, there's nothing you can do to hurt me." Castellan said. "And with Heinrich dead, there is no way you can get another."

Castellan tried to grab Alexander, to which Alexander dodged, and ripped out the Blade from Castellan's stomach. As the Blade left his body, Castellan's wounds instantly healed. Alexander backed up, and Castellan instantly appeared in front of him, ready to attack. Alexander dodged the attack and stabbed Castellan in the leg. Just like before, it had no effect. Alexander quickly backed up and tried attacking Castellan from the back. Castellan slightly scraped his scythe against the ground, creating a massive shockwave that forced Alexander away.

Alexander got back up and tried attacking again. Each of his attacks were either blocked by Castellan, or simply had no effect. Alexander attacked faster and faster, screaming in rage. Eventually there was another loud explosion from Alexander, just like the ones from his first fight with Castellan, and his fight against the Husks on the floating village. No matter what, Alexander couldn't do anything. Eventually he fell to the floor in exhaustion. He couldn't walk anymore, as his legs were completely shattered.

Castellan approached Alexander, and laughed at his pathetic state. Castellan raised his scythe slightly, and tried stabbing Alexander. Alexander blocked with the Blade as he couldn't dodge. As the Scythe and Blade met each other, there was a giant shockwave. Alexander looked in horror to see the Blade completely shattered.

"Do you still think you can win?" Castellan said. "Your friends are gone, your strength is gone, your weapon is gone!"

Alexander tried using Sorcery, but the image of Erwins Husk still haunted him.

"I can feel your failed attempts at sorcery." Said Castellan. "Each time you fail to use it, I feel like I've won just a little bit more."

Castellan raised his scythe in the air, ready to kill Alexander. Heinrich's last words came back to Alexander. As the Scythe grew closer to his body, Alexander imagined a world without Castellan. A future world where Castellan died in this fight, a perfect world. Right before the scythe hit him, Alexander felt something inside. He felt the image of Erwins Husk fade away, the past fade away. Alexander tried one last time to use sorcery.

Castellan froze in place. Not just Castellan, but the smoke and dust around them, the birds in the air, the insects on the ground, it all stopped. Only Alexander could keep moving. Alexander moved behind Castellan, and everything resumed. As the Scythe hit the ground, Castellan was shocked to see Alexander not beneath him in pieces.

"Can you still feel it?" Alexander said. "My failed attempts at Sorcery, can you still feel them?"

Castellan quickly turned around and tried attacking Alexander again. Just like before, the world froze for Alexander to move behind him.

"Do you still feel like you've won?" Alexander said. For the first time in his life, Castellan felt afraid.

"What the Hell is this?" Castellan said.

"This is the power I couldn't use before." Alexander said. Castellan tried attacking Alexander again. Alexander gathered a purple energy in his hands, and launched it at Castellan, throwing him back several meters.

"During my time with the Council, I learned how to use Omnipotence." Alexander said. "And during my time hiding from you, I learned how to use Time Control. Before, I couldn't use them even though I knew how to. Now, I can use them to their fullest extent."

Alexander grabbed the handle of the shattered Blade, and casted a spell. The broken fragments came back together, making the Blade as if it had never been shattered.

"Heinrich taught me something special," Alexander said. "He taught me how I can use Time Control to kill you. By reverting you back to your old self, I can strip away your Immortality, and make you human again."

Alexander gathered a green energy in his hands, as Castellan attempted to attack him again. As the green energy hit him, Castellan could feel himself weakening. The world no longer shaped beneath his feet, lions would no longer shrivel in fear at just his sight, he could feel himself slowly dying.

"What did you do to me," Castellan yelled in fear.

"I reverted you to your old self." Alexander said. "You're now the same as when you never used sorcery. Now, you can die."

Alexander stood above the now pathetic Castellan, and raised his Blade.

I can feel you with me. Alexander thought to himself. *I can feel your spirits behind me, giving me strength. All the friends I made, all the victims of this psychopath. Frieda, Heinrich, Thomas, Kayla, Erwin, and the thousands of others Castellan has unlawfully killed. Your spirits are with me, waiting for this to end. You may move on to the afterlife now, this is over now.*

Alexander used Time Control to accelerate his Blade. It became so fast that the fiction against the air set it ablaze, and so fast that it hit Castellan before he could even see it. The Blade hit the ground with so much force, it created an explosion equal to 100,000 kilograms of Gunpowder. The entire kingdom shook, and the surrounding villages could see the explosion and feel the heat. As the explosion cleared out,

Alexander found himself in a giant crater. Castellan's body was completely vaporized. With him dead, all the Husks would also cease to live. Alexander had purified the world by erasing this evil once and for all.

Alexander was suddenly hit by a revelation. He grabbed the Blade, filled it with green energy, and raised it into the ground.

I can bring them back. He thought to himself. *With Time Control, I can revive them all!*

Right before he casted the spell, Alexander stopped. *No, it wouldn't be right.* He thought to himself. *They wouldn't want it, they lived their lives and died honorable deaths. I should let them go, let them move on to the afterlife.* Alexander let go of the spell he placed on the Blade, shattering it.

"Goodbye." He said to the Blade. "Your purpose was to rid the world of Castellan, and you've served that purpose well. It's time for you to move on as well."

Alexander used a spell to bury the Blade underground. He stood up, and began walking back towards the Ruins of the Council building.

Chapter Nine: Oh, how the world has changed!

San Diego California, USA, August 1st 2022;

Alexander sat in a helicopter, surrounded by soldiers. One soldier finally decided to speak out to break the awkward silence.

"Is it true you're 400 years old?" He said.

Alexander chuckled. "Yes. After I rebuilt the Council and created Fate Control, I stripped away my fate, so I can't die until I say so."

"What's Fate Control," the soldier said.

"The combination of Omnipotence and Time Control." Alexander said. "It's exactly how it sounds. I can control people's fate. I can give people a new fate, and the universe will enforce it. I can simply decide something, and the universe will work to make it true."

"So, you're like a God?" The soldier said.

"I'm the closest there is, other than the true God."

"Alexander, you're up" a voice said over the radio.

"I'll see you all later." Alexander said, before appearing right outside the Helicopter.

Alexander saw a horrible sight. The city of San Diego was in complete ruins. Sorcerers had completely overtaken it.

"Maybe re-introducing Sorcery to the world was a mistake." Alexander said.

An attack helicopter spotted Alexander, and began hovering next to him. *I have decided that the helicopter's engine will explode.* Alexander thought to himself. The helicopter suddenly engulfed in flames, as the engine suddenly blew up, killing everyone on board.

The water shook and rippled. Suddenly, a Giant Stone Golem appeared. Alexander seemed to recognize it.

They're utilizing Heinrich's old spells. But instead of making a stone dragon, they made a stone giant.

“If you will use Heinrich's spells against me, I'll also use them against you.” Alexander said. “The spell that killed Heinrich, that's what I'll use. Re-inventing it so I could use it without killing myself and instead targeting my enemies, that's one of the first things I did. After killing Castellan.”

Black Energy surrounded Alexander, before the crystals materialized around the stone giant, and every sorcerer in the city. As the Spell was let off, every single sorcery was erased from the world, with no unintended damage.

“You don't seem to understand,” Alexander said, “I've dedicated my entire life towards ridding the world of all evil, and none shall stand in my way. None shall hurt the innocent so long as I am still here.”

Mystic Blade, The End

Milton Keynes UK
Ingram Content Group UK Ltd.
UKHW020840290324
440175UK00001B/110

9 798224 560769